Toby Bunny's Secret Hiding Place

By Dave Werner
Illustrated by James Spence

A GOLDEN BOOK · NEW YORK
Western Publishing Company, Inc., Racine, Wisconsin 53404

Little Toby Bunny liked to romp and play
with his big brothers and sisters.
Sometimes they gave him horsey rides.

Other times they pulled him around the
yard in a little red wagon.

But when they played tag, Toby couldn't keep up with them.

And when they played catch, Toby couldn't throw the ball far enough.

So one morning Toby decided that he would play by himself. He went looking for a secret hiding place.

The linen closet looked like a good place to hide. It was nice and dark inside.

Toby put on his space goggles and got out his glowzoids. He pretended he was captain of his own spaceship. Just when he reached the glowzoids' galaxy, the closet door burst open.

"TOBY!" cried his mommy. "You know you're not allowed to play in the closet! Come out of there—right now!"

"Sorry, Mommy," said Toby.

Toby looked around the house for another hiding place. The tablecloth on the dining room table nearly reached the floor. Toby thought, "This will make a good tent."

He lifted up the tablecloth and scooted under the table.

Toby felt very cozy. He lay there
listening for coyotes and hoot owls.
Suddenly a bright red ball bounced into
the tent. It was followed by his twin sisters,
Berry and Merry.

They liked the tent so much that they
stayed to play house.
   "You can be the baby, Toby," said Merry.

"Time for your bottle," said Berry.
"Yuck!" Toby exclaimed.

Toby ran outside. He did not stop until
he got to the bottom of the hill, where the
grass grew taller than his head and there
were a lot of trees.

He imagined that he was an explorer
deep in a jungle.

"Look out below! Geeeronimoooo!" yelled his brothers, Darryl and Mookie.

Toby looked up just in time to see them pretend-parachute from a limb overhead.

THUD—KA-THUNK! They landed on either side of Toby.

"Aha!" exclaimed Mookie as he grabbed Toby. "We've caught a spy!"

"Let's take him prisoner!" teased Darryl.

Quickly Toby broke free of his brothers and ran up over the hill to the edge of the forest, where a large blackberry patch grew.

He saw a small opening. It looked just the right size for a little bunny. "No one will find me here," he thought.

But the opening was smaller than it looked.

Toby's fur caught on the prickly-sharp thorns. He couldn't move forward, and he couldn't move backward.

Only his little white cottontail stuck out of the patch like a flag.

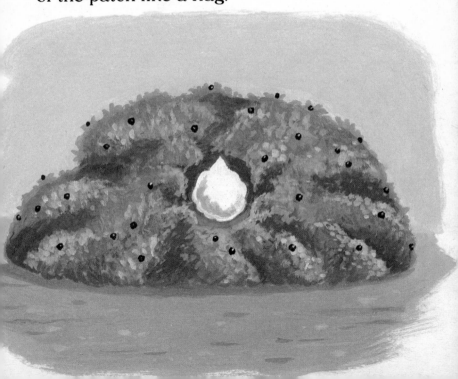

"Help! Help!" yelled Toby. But no one came.

It was dark in the blackberry patch. Tears trickled down Toby's cheeks.

Luckily, just then, Toby's daddy came walking by. He couldn't miss seeing the white cottontail sticking out of the patch.

"That fuzzy little tail looks familiar," he said. "Toby?"

Poor Toby could only twitch his tail in reply.

Very gently his daddy pulled the
blackberry twigs apart so Toby could
wiggle free.

"Daddy, Daddy!" Toby sobbed with
relief.

His daddy picked him up and brushed
away his tears.

"Why, Toby," he said, "what were you
doing in the blackberry patch?"

"I just wanted to find a secret hiding
place," Toby blurted out.

"We all need a secret hiding place
sometimes," said Daddy. "I know just the
place for you."

Toby's daddy carried him piggyback down a narrow garden path. At the end there was a maple tree. And tied to one of the branches was a hammock.

"Can you keep a secret?" asked Daddy.
Toby nodded his head.

"This is *my* secret hiding place," Daddy
said. "If you like it, it can be yours, too."

Toby and his daddy climbed in the hammock and rocked back and forth.

"You mean we can have a secret hiding place *together*?" asked Toby.

"That's right," said Daddy. "It can be *our* secret hiding place."

Toby's face broke into a big smile as he gave his daddy the biggest hug ever.

Toby and his daddy went to the secret hiding place many, many times.

And sometimes Toby went alone.